HOW TO
MAKE FRIENDS
WITH A GHOST

WRITTEN AND ILLUSTRATED BY REBECCA GREEN

ANDERSEN PRESS

IF YOU'VE EVER BEEN FRIGHTENED BY A GHOST, THE THOUGHT OF BECOMING FRIENDS WITH ONE MIGHT SEEM AWFULLY SCARY.

BUT I ASSURE YOU, GHOSTS ARE SWEET CREATURES WHO NEED FRIENDS TOO. AND WHO BETTER TO BEFRIEND THEM THAN YOU?

THIS HELPFUL GUIDE WILL SHOW YOU HOW TO CREATE A LIFELONG (AND BEYOND) FRIENDSHIP!

GHOSTS ARE TRICKY TO TRACK DOWN, SO IT IS ADVISABLE
THAT YOU DO NOT TRY TO LOOK FOR ONE.

MOST OF THE TIME, WHEN A PERSON THINKS THEY HAVE
FOUND A GHOST, THEY HAVE NOT (SEE FIG. 1, FIG. 2, FIG. 3).

FIG. 1: COSTUMED CHILD   FIG. 2: DUSTY CAMERA LENS   FIG. 3: TOWEL ON A DOORKNOB

HOWEVER, DR PHANTONEOUS SPOOKEL,
LEADING GHOST EXPERT AND POET, WRITES:

A GHOST IS NEARLY IMPOSSIBLE TO FIND.
YOU CAN LOOK TILL YOUR FACE TURNS BLUE.
BUT IF YOU'RE A PERSON WHO IS SWEET, WARM AND KIND,
A GHOST MAY COME OUT AND FIND YOU.

IF YOU THINK YOU HAVE BEEN FOUND BY A GHOST,
USE THIS HANDY CLASSIFICATION GUIDE* TO MAKE SURE
THE CREATURE IN QUESTION IS, IN FACT, A GHOST.

*FROM THE ARCHIVES OF THE DEPARTMENT OF PARANORMAL CLASSIFICATION
AT THE SOCIETY OF SUPERNATURAL STUDIES.

PART 1

GHOST
BASICS

ALTHOUGH YOU MIGHT BE FRIGHTENED WHEN A GHOST GREETS
YOU, DO NOT RUN! GHOSTS ARE VERY SENSITIVE CREATURES.

SIMPLY SMILE, WAVE
AND TELL THE GHOST YOUR NAME.

ONCE THE GHOST KNOWS YOU ARE FRIENDLY,
IT WILL MOST LIKELY FOLLOW YOU.

WELCOME THE GHOST INTO YOUR HOME.
IF IT IS RELUCTANT, A SIMPLE BLOW WILL GET THE GHOST INSIDE.

WARNING: NEVER _EVER_ PUT YOUR HAND THROUGH A GHOST.
IT CAN CAUSE A SERIOUS TUMMY ACHE.

PART 2

GHOST
CARE

CINNAMON-DUSTED
INSECTS

MOULDY TOAST

EARWAX TRUFFLES

MUD TARTS

PICKLED
BOGIES

GHOSTS LOVE TO SNACK. ONE SURE WAY
TO A GHOST'S HEART IS TO FIX ITS FAVOURITE TREATS.

CHANCES ARE, YOUR GHOST WILL WANT TO HELP YOU IN THE KITCHEN.
I SUGGEST MAKING FLOATING SPAGHETTI AND MUDBALLS TOGETHER!

COOK TIME: ALL DAY | SERVES: ONE HUNGRY GHOST*

1 CUP DRIED WITCH HAIR
2 CUPS CREEK WATER
¾ CUP MUD (ANY VARIETY)
¾ CUP TOMATO SAUCE
2 TSP SPIDER-EGG PARMESAN

1. BOIL WITCH HAIR FOR SIX HOURS.
2. ROLL MUD INTO BALLS AND
   REFRIGERATE FOR TWO HOURS.
3. DRAIN HAIR, ADD TOMATO SAUCE AND
   MUDBALLS.
4. FLOAT AND COMBINE THE PASTA.
5. TOP WITH SPIDER-EGG PARMESAN.

*LEFTOVERS WILL KEEP IN THE REFRIGERATOR FOR UP TO THREE YEARS.

I ALSO RECOMMEND THESE OTHER TASTY DISHES!*

MUSTY BISCUITS
WITH TOE JAM

MONSTER-MASHED
POTATOES

DEAD LEAF SALAD WITH
BOO-TONS

SPIDERWEB SUSHI

THUNDERSTORM
SOUP

*FOR THESE AND MORE RECIPES, SEE MY BOOK
SUPERSTITIOUS AND NUTRITIOUS: WACKY SNACKIES FOR YOUR GHOST.

TAKE YOUR GHOST FOR A WALK IN THE WOODS.
GHOSTS LOVE TO COLLECT LEAVES, ACORNS AND WORMS.

READ SCARY STORIES TOGETHER. GHOSTS LOVE TO BE READ TO.
I SUGGEST *TALES OF THE LIVING* BY MORT L. BINGS.

TELL JOKES TO YOUR GHOST! THEY LOVE TO GIGGLE!

"KNOCK, KNOCK!"

"WHO'S THERE?"

"BOO!"

"BOO WHO?"

"WHY ARE YOU CRYING?!"

TAKE YOUR GHOST TRICK-OR-TREATING ON HALLOWEEN.
EVERYONE WILL THINK IT'S A GHOST COSTUME!

THROW A DANCE PARTY! GHOSTS LIKE TO GROOVE TO
CREEPY MUSIC. I RECOMMEND *SPOOKY JAMS* BY THE SPIDERZ.

GIVE YOUR GHOST A BEDTIME BATH! I SUGGEST WARMING
WATER IN A CAULDRON AND BLOWING YOUR OWN BUBBLES.

PUTTING YOUR GHOST TO BED EVERY NIGHT WILL
ENSURE IT SLEEPS SOUNDLY WITH PLENTY OF NIGHTMARES!
GHOSTS LOVE NIGHTMARES.

MAKE YOUR GHOST A COSY BED. TRY LAYING DOWN MOSS
IN THE DARKEST CORNER OF THE ATTIC. YOU CAN ALSO
MAKE A CANOPY OUT OF SPIDERWEBS!

GHOSTS LOVE TO BE SUNG TO. INSTEAD OF WORDS,
TRY SINGING TO THEM IN EERIE HUMS AND WAILS.

OTHERS MIGHT BE WARY AROUND YOUR GHOST,
SO IT'S BEST TO FIND GOOD HIDING SPOTS.

YOU CAN HIDE YOUR GHOST IN A TISSUE BOX...

OR HIDE YOUR GHOST IN YOUR SOCK DRAWER!
(IT'S ALSO A GREAT PLACE FOR NAPPING.)

YOU CAN EVEN HIDE YOUR GHOST IN THE REFRIGERATOR.
GHOSTS LOVE TO BE COLD.

DO NOT LET YOUR GHOST BE USED AS A TISSUE!
BOGIE REMOVAL IS NEVER EASY!*

*FOR CLEANING TIPS, SEE MY BOOK
FROM GROSS TO BOAST: GROOMING TIPS FOR YOUR GHOST.

DO NOT LET YOUR GHOST HELP WITH THE LAUNDRY!

DO NOT LET YOUR GHOST GET EATEN!
OTHERS CAN MISTAKE GHOSTS FOR FOOD ITEMS,
SUCH AS EGGS, WHIPPED CREAM, SOUR CREAM AND MARSHMALLOWS.

PART 3

GROWING
TOGETHER

WHEN YOU MOVE TO A NEW HOME, MAKE SURE IT'S NOT ALREADY HAUNTED.
GHOSTS DO NOT LIKE COMPETITION.

WHEN YOU START WORKING,
YOU WILL STILL HAVE TO MAKE TIME FOR YOUR GHOST.

I SUGGEST A "TAKE YOUR GHOST TO WORK" DAY.

WHEN YOU START A FAMILY,
YOUR GHOST WILL LOVE MINI VERSIONS OF YOU TOO.

NOTE: GHOSTS LOVE TO PLAY PEEK-A-BOO!

YOU WILL GET OLD BUT YOUR GHOST NEVER WILL.
IT WILL STILL WANT TO COLLECT LEAVES, ACORNS AND WORMS.

IF YOUR EYES CAN NO LONGER SEE,
YOUR GHOST WILL BE THERE TO READ TO YOU.

AND EVEN IF YOU CAN'T REMEMBER JOKES, YOUR GHOST CAN.
IT WILL BE THERE TO MAKE YOU LAUGH.

THE BEST PART ABOUT MAKING FRIENDS WITH A GHOST IS
THAT YOU'LL HAVE THE SWEETEST FRIEND... FOREVER!

ACCORDING TO DR PHANTONEOUS SPOOKEL:

IF YOU'VE BEEN LUCKY ENOUGH TO BE FOUND
BY A GHOST THAT CALLS YOU ITS FRIEND,
THEN YOUR FRIENDSHIP WILL LAST,
FOR IT KNOWS NO BOUNDS —
YOU'LL BE FRIENDS EVEN AFTER THE END.

FOR MATTHEW PHELPS, MY IDEAS GUY
AND PERSONAL PANCAKE CHEF

ALSO, IN LOVING MEMORY OF THE
SWEETEST AND MOST BRILLIANT
GHOST, MISS EMOGENE NAGEL

A HUGE THANK-YOU TO TARA AND
JESSICA WHO BELIEVED IN THIS LITTLE
GHOST AND WORKED SO HARD TO
BRING THE BOOK TO LIFE

REBECCA GREEN IS AN ILLUSTRATOR, PAINTER
AND MAKE-BELIEVE MAKER WHO SPENDS HER DAYS
(AND SOMETIMES NIGHTS) ILLUSTRATING FOR
CHILDREN'S AND YOUNG ADULT BOOKS, MAGAZINES
AND GALLERIES. WHILE SHE WOULD NOT DESCRIBE
HERSELF AS BRAVE, SHE LOVES ALL THINGS SPOOKY
AND MYSTERIOUS. **HOW TO MAKE FRIENDS WITH
A GHOST** IS HER FIRST PICTURE BOOK. SHE LIVES IN
NASHVILLE, TENNESSEE.

THIS PAPERBACK EDITION FIRST PUBLISHED IN GREAT BRITAIN IN
2018 BY ANDERSEN PRESS LTD.,
20 VAUXHALL BRIDGE ROAD, LONDON SW1V 2SA

COPYRIGHT © 2017 BY REBECCA GREEN.

PUBLISHED BY ARRANGEMENT WITH TUNDRA BOOKS, A DIVISION
OF PENGUIN RANDOM HOUSE CANADA LIMITED.

THE RIGHT OF REBECCA GREEN TO BE IDENTIFIED AS THE
AUTHOR AND ILLUSTRATOR OF THIS WORK HAS BEEN ASSERTED
BY HER IN ACCORDANCE WITH THE COPYRIGHT, DESIGNS AND
PATENTS ACT, 1988. ALL RIGHTS RESERVED.
PRINTED AND BOUND IN CHINA.

10   9   8   7   6   5   4   3   2   1

BRITISH LIBRARY CATALOGUING IN PUBLICATION DATA AVAILABLE.
ISBN 978 1 78344 680 3